A Rookie reader® TREASURY

Quite Enough Hot Dogs

and Other
Silly Stories

Children's Press®
An Imprint of Scholastic Inc.
New York • Toronto • London • Auckland • Sydney
Mexico City • New Delhi • Hong Kong
Danbury, Connecticut

Dear Rookie Reader,

Watch Out!
Here come **bubbles** that are
trouble! See a **hot dog** run!
What other silly things happen?
Find out! Read these stories.

Have fun and keep reading!

P.S. Don't forget to check out the
fun activities on pages 124—127.

Contents

Bubble Trouble

By Joy N. Hulme

Illustrated by Mike Cressy

Dip the stick in bubble stuff.

give a slow and steady puff.

Oh! Oh!

See them grow.

How they flow,

and glow and go,

fast

and slow.

Watch them fly
in the sky,

and high.

Oh, oh, bubble trouble.

Stop! Stop! Don't pop!

No, no, not that!

SPLAT!

Do not sigh.

Do not cry.

Bubbles come

and bubbles go.

Dip the stick again and blow.

All Wrapped up

By Thera S. Callahan

Illustrated by Mike Gordon

It is Dad's birthday.

We have his gift,
but there is no tape.

We could use
gummy glue sticks,

or fluffy frosting,

or baby bandages,

or slippery syrup,

or gooey gum,

or mushy marshmallows,

or runny honey,

or sticky stamps,

or tacky taffy,

or jiggly jelly.

What would work best?
We did not know.

So we used a little of
this and a little of that.

And the paper stuck.

Jordan's Sick Silly Day

By Justine Fontes

Illustrated by Jared Lee

I am sick. That's no fun!

I can't play outside.
I can't see my friends.

I am wheezing
and sneezing.

The worst part of staying home is being bored!

Then I remember something.
I can use my imagination!

I pretend my Teddy bear
can play cards.

I let Teddy win.

I try to build a house of cards.
Then I wonder.

What if I lived in a real house
of cards?

A monster blows down my house!

So I build a house of blocks.

The monster kicks down
my house of blocks.

So I build a house of books.

That stops the monster,
because he can't read.

I take a sip of orange juice.

I pretend I'm floating down an orange river.

I can't be in school with my friends today.

But I sure am having lots of fun.

What shall I imagine next?

I imagine I am feeling better.

Guess what? It's working!

Quite Enough Hot Dogs

By Wil Mara

Illustrated by Pete Whitehead

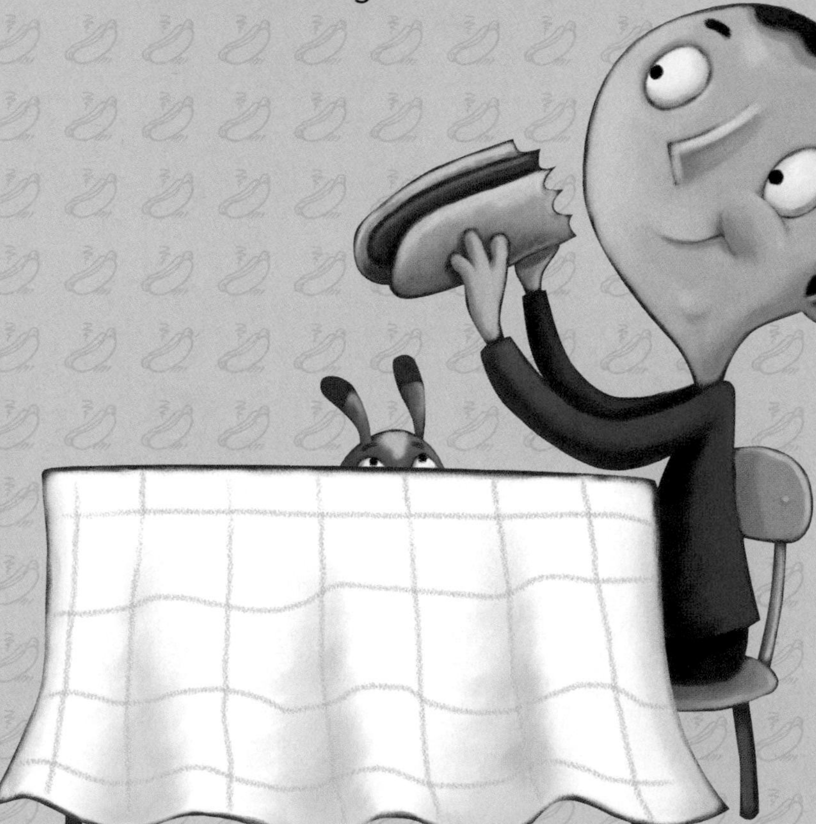

"What can I eat?" asked Steve.
"I know! Please make one more hot dog!"

"Ugh," said Mom. "You are going
to turn into a huge hot dog!"
Steve laughed and took another bite.

But Steve's stomach ached
after eating all those hot dogs.
He decided to sleep for a while.

When Steve woke, he could smell the scent of hot dogs. Mmmmm . . .

But he could not get up!
Steve fell to the floor.

He faced the mirror.
Eek! Steve had turned into a hot dog!

"Mom! Something is quite wrong!"
Steve cried tears of yellow mustard.

He wiggled down the stairs.
"Mom! Help!"

Mom wasn't there, but
someone else was.

It was Steve's dog Nate.
Nate loved hot dogs, too!

Nate wagged his tail.
"No, Nate, no!" Steve cried.
Nate ran after him.

Steve made his way to the backyard, but Nate chased him.

Steve couldn't escape!
Nate leapt into the air
with his mouth wide open.

"No!" Steve screamed.
But just before Nate took
a bite, Steve woke up.

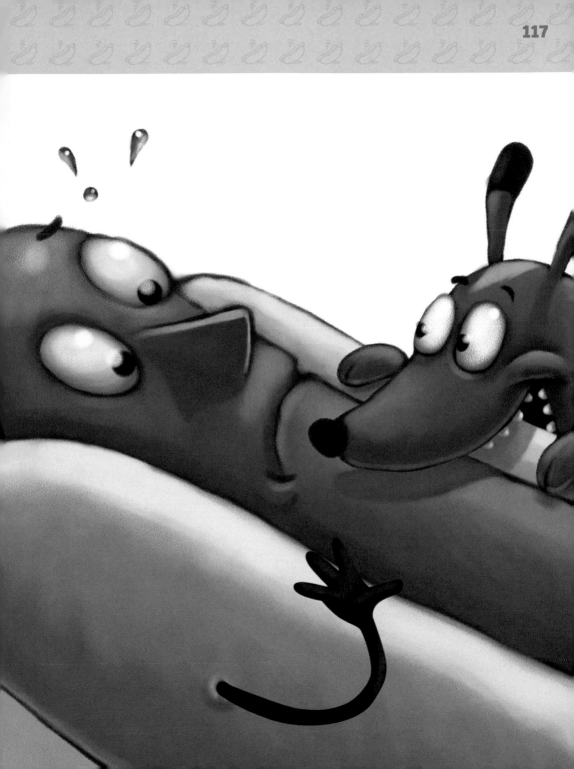

Steve raced to the mirror.
Now he knew it had all been a dream!

Steve went down to the kitchen.
"What about another hot dog?"
asked Mom.
"No!" Steve answered.

"But I thought you liked hot dogs!"

"I guess I changed my mind!"

Rhyme Time!

Match each word with its rhyme.

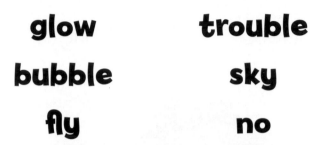

glow   **trouble**

bubble   **sky**

fly   **no**

What rhymes with **_pop_**?
Hint: there is a clue in this picture...
Can you think of more rhymes?

Silly and Sticky!

What silly, sticky things can
you think of?
Make your own list.
Draw pictures, too!

Match the words and pictures.

books　　　**monster**　　　**Teddy bear**

Make up your own silly story!
Think of something new for Jordan
and the monster to do!

These pictures are all mixed up!
Tell what happened first, second,
third, and last!

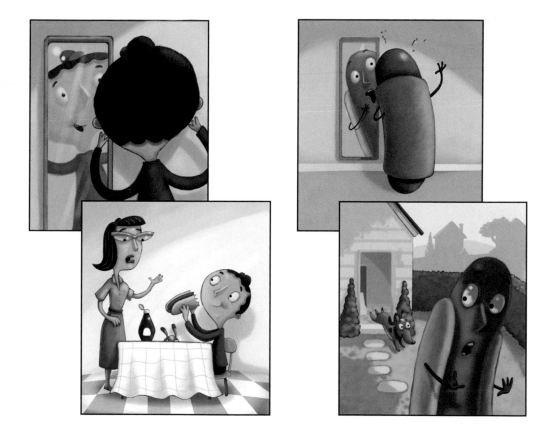

Tell about the story.
What part did you like best?

Library of Congress Cataloging-in-Publication Data

Quite enough hot dogs and other silly stories.
   v. cm. -- (A Rookie reader treasury)
  Contents: Bubble trouble / by Joy N. Hulme ; illustrated by Mike Cressy
          All wrapped up / by Thera S. Callahan ; illustrated by Mike Gordon
          Jordan's silly sick day / by Justine Fontes ; illustrated By Jared Lee
          Quite enough hot dogs / by Wil Mara ; illustrated by Pete Whitehead.
    ISBN-13: 978-0-531-21728-3
    ISBN-10: 0-531-21728-0

  1. Children's stories, American. [1. Short stories.]
II. Title. III. Series.

PZ5.Q46 2008
[E]--dc22   2008008293

Cover top right, TOC top left, and illustrations pages 4-33, 124 © 1999 Mike Cressy
Cover bottom left, TOC bottom left, and illustrations pages 64-93, 126 © 2004 Jared Lee
Cover top left, Title Page, TOC bottom right, and illustrations pages 94-123, 127 © 2007 Pete Whitehead
Cover bottom right, TOC top right, and illustrations pages 34-63, 125 © 2003 Mike Gordon.

1 2 3 4 5 6 7 8 9 10 R 18 17 16 15 14 13 12 11 10 09